THE MUPPETS

Little, Brown and Company

Hachette Book Group
237 Park Avenue, New York, NY 10017
Visit our website at www.lb-kids.com

Little, Brown and Company is a division of Hachette Book Group, Inc.
The Little, Brown name and logo are trademarks of Hachette Book Group, Inc.

The publisher is not responsible for websites (or their content) that are not owned by the publisher.

First Edition: October 2012
ISBN 978-0-316-20132-2

10 9 8 7 6 5 4 3 2 1

CW

Printed in the United States of America

Book design by Maria Mercado

THE MUPPETS

The Twelve Days of a Muppet Christmas

And a Chicken in a Pine Tree

by Martha T. Ottersley
illustrated by Amy Mebberson

LITTLE, BROWN AND COMPANY
New York Boston

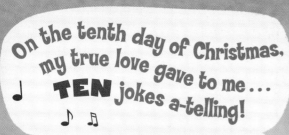

On the tenth day of Christmas, my true love gave to me . . . **TEN** jokes a-telling!

What did the Christmas tree say to the other Christmas tree?

Wocka! Wocka!

PENNY FOR THE BEAR!

On the twelfth day of Christmas, my true love gave to me . . .